Date Due

NOV 2 6	APR 17 '91	DEC 5 '91	MAY 27 '92		
DEC 18 '90	APR 9	DEC 19 '91			
DEC 2 1 '90	APR 2 9	FEB 24	FEB 2 '93		
JAN 2 2 '91	MAY 6	MAR 10 '92	FEB 10 '93		
JAN 3 0 '91	MAY 21 '91	MAR 19 '92	FEB 22		
FEB 28 '91	OCT 29 '91	APR 1 '92	MAR 4 '93		
MAR 4 '91	NOV 5 '91	APR 22 '92			
MAR 14 '91	NOV 13 '91	APR 23 '92			
MAR 26 '91	NOV 27 '91	MAY 19 '92			

BRODART, INC. Cat. No. 23 231 Printed in U.S.A.

P9-ECO-299

```
E       Zolotow, Charlotte
Zol     The quiet mother and the
        noisy little boy
```

NEIL ~~CUMMINS~~ SCHOOL LIBRARY
CORTE MADERA, CALIF.

THE QUIET MOTHER
and the
NOISY LITTLE BOY

Charlotte Zolotow
Illustrations by Marc Simont

Harper & Row, Publishers

RARY

The Quiet Mother and the Noisy Little Boy
Text copyright © 1953, 1989 by Charlotte Zolotow
Illustrations copyright © 1989 by Marc Simont
Another version of this text first published in 1953 by Lothrop, Lee & Shepard Co., Inc.

Printed in the U.S.A. All rights reserved.

1 2 3 4 5 6 7 8 9 10

Newly Illustrated Edition

Library of Congress Cataloging-in-Publication Data
Zolotow, Charlotte, 1915–
    The quiet mother and the noisy little boy / Charlotte Zolotow : illustrated by Marc
Simont.
        p.   cm.
    Summary: A noisy little boy discovers the pleasure of a quiet moment with his
mother after his very noisy cousin pays a visit to their house.
    ISBN 0-06-026978-2 : $ ISBN 0-06-026979-0 (lib. bdg.) : $
    [1. Noise—Fiction. 2. Mothers and sons—Fiction.] I. Simont, Marc, ill. II. Title.
PZ7.Z77Qi 1989
[E]—dc 19   88-936
                                                                                    CIP
                                                                                    AC

THE QUIET MOTHER
and the
NOISY LITTLE BOY

Once there was a little boy who liked noise.
It was part of him and he made it all the time.
He talked to his mother in his loudest voice.
He talked to his father in his loudest voice.
He talked to his little brown dog in his loudest voice.

And long before the mother and father got up each morning, he talked to himself in his loud little boy voice. And long after he should have been asleep at night, the mother heard her little boy's voice talking talking talking loudly to himself.

The little boy liked his records played loudly, and watched television loudly, and played with the little dog loudly. He did everything so loudly his mother always knew what he was doing even though they were in different parts of the house.

Scritttttch. "His top drawer," Sandy's mother said one morning.

Scraaaaaapppe. He's closed it now, she thought to herself.

Then a little scattered sound like a box and lid falling from the shelf.

His cap, she thought.

Then a metallic ringing clatter like a clothes hanger knocked on the floor.

His sweater.

Clunkety clunkety clunkety CLUNK.

He's downstairs.

Crash! The swinging door between the kitchen and the dining room went on swinging back and forth long after the little boy had streaked through the kitchen and the back door had gone ke-bang behind him.

Now the mother could hear the little boy's shouts from the garden, rising above the barking of the little brown dog who was so glad to be with him.

"Oh, I wish I liked noise," the mother said, holding her head. "I want a life without noise."

"You'd miss it," the father said, smiling.

But the mother didn't think so.

There were only two things the little boy was quiet for, and those were his books and his puzzles.

One morning, just as the little boy settled on the floor in the living room to put a new puzzle together, his father took him off in the car to visit his cousin Roger. Roger and his family had just moved to town. Sandy hadn't seen Roger's house. Roger hadn't seen his.

"I'll bring them both back after lunch," Sandy's father said as Sandy kissed his mother good-by.

"Enjoy the quiet," the father said, smiling.

When they left, the mother took a cup of coffee and sat down in the quiet living room.

How lovely, she thought.

The coffee was warm and good and the quietness was everywhere, as though the world were standing still. After a while she began to feel strange.

The plants in the living room seemed quieter than usual. The turned-off phonograph and the blank television looked lonely. The stairs looked empty and quieter than stairs are supposed to look.

The books in the bookshelves, the screens in all the doors, looked quiet. And the mother walked through the house as though it belonged to someone else. As the morning wore on she listened to the quietness all around. She opened her book to read but something disturbed her.

The only sound she heard was the clock ticking away the time.

NEIL CUMMINS SCHOOL LIBRARY
CORTE MADERA, CALIF.

What can be the matter? she thought.

And the answer came immediately.

"I miss my little boy," she said.

And just then there were car doors banging outside. Sandy and Roger and Sandy's father were home. There was a scuff skiffle scuff scripp scripp up the back walk and Sandy came bounding into her arms.

"Hey, Mom. Roger's come to our house now."

"How nice," his mother said. And she started to say something else but she suddenly sat up and put her hand on her heart. Roger was shouting more loudly than even Sandy could shout.

"I LIKE YOUR HOUSE AND MOTHER SENDS
LOVE AND SHE'LL HONK FOR ME AT FIVE."

Sandy looked down at the puzzle on the floor
where he'd left it.

"Roger," he said, "come on, let's finish this
puzzle."

"NOT NOW," shouted Roger. "LET'S DO ELECTRIC
TRAINS."

Sandy's mother usually had a soft voice, but she
spoke loudly so that she could be heard.

"I bet Roger would like that new cowboy book
of yours," she said.

Sandy went upstairs to find the book, but before
he could open it Roger began to shout:

YAAAAAAAAAAAAAA!

"COWBOY YIP YIIIIIII YAAAAAAAAAAA," and he galloped off out of the room. The whole house seemed to shake, and in the bedroom something heavy clattered to the floor. There was a breaking shattering sound as the pieces went all over.

OAAAARRRRRRD!

"Oh," said Sandy's mother, "I'm sure the living room ceiling must have cracked." But before she could go see, Roger had grown tired of being a cowboy. He had found the electric trains! Instead of the usual click clack around the track and the whistle whistling at the stops, he was shouting in a voice loud as thunder:

"ALL ABOOOOOAAAARRRRRD
FOR ALL POINTS EAST AND WEST,
FOR CHICAGO, CHATTANOOGA,
NEW YORK AND EUROPE.
ALL ABOOOOOAAAARRRRRD...."

Sandy's mother could hardly hear the horn an hour later when it went honk honk honk. But Roger heard.

"G'D-BY," he shouted.

There was a sound like dynamite exploding and Roger raced down the stairs, glumpety glumpety glumpety glump.

"G'D-BY, THANK YOU, G'D-BY," he called again, hanging out the window, waving wildly as the car drove away.

Sandy had followed him downstairs. He stood at the door and waved back. Then he sighed. He closed the screen door, which was hanging open, carefully behind him. The little brown dog pattered up behind him.

Sandy looked at his mother. She looked tired.
His mother looked at Sandy.
"Whewwwww," Sandy said. "Roger is noisy!"
"Yes, he is," his mother agreed.
Sandy looked at his puzzle on the floor.
"Some things you need quiet for," he said.
· He was thinking of all the times he'd heard his
mother say, "I wish I liked noise."

He was deciding never to be noisy again.

But his mother guessed what he was thinking.

She remembered how quiet it had been in the house without him.

"Both are good," she said quickly. "Quietness and noise at different times for different things. It can be too quiet or too noisy if there is too much of either."

They knelt together to pick up the pieces of the puzzle, putting them back in the box, gently, one by one. The little brown dog watched them and wagged his tail.

Sandy's mother looked at him and smiled. He smiled back. And neither of them said a word.